Good Home Cookin'

Christian Burch

* * *

To my wife Carly for never giving up on me. Also for your good home cookin'. I do love it!

* * *

TABLE OF CONTENTS

Books by Christian Burch

E.V.I.L. (Re-release 2023)
A Sinking Feeling (Re-release 2023)
Haunted (Re-Release October 2022)
Haunted II: Awakening (Re-release Fall 2023)
Dark Horizons (Re-release August 2022)
Dark Horizons: Legends (Summer 2023)
E.V.I.L. 2: Regeneration (TBD)
Approaching Darkness (TBD)

Our Family Recipe
Good Home Cookin'
For Here Or To Go (April 2022)
Our Family Recipe (June 2022)
Secret Ingredient (Spring 2023)

Shattered Dimensions
Cuddle Time (May 2022)

PROLOGUE

May 16th, 1996

The two detectives exited their car and prepared to make their way through the throng of reporters congregated outside the prison. Detective Corder counted fifteen cameras and at least double the number of reporters from the various news stations. The scent of lilac and fresh soap brought a smile to his face. He'd dropped off his uniform at Gemini Twins Dry Cleaning to be cleaned and pressed. Those two women didn't disappoint, and he'd left them a decent tip. His uniform hadn't been this nice since the first few months after graduating the academy.

A sigh from the man standing next to him brought his attention to his attire. Either Davis didn't care about how his appearance in front of so many reporters, and cameras which would then put his image in front of possibly millions of eyes. He smelled of stale cigarettes and body odor. Corder couldn't help but wonder if he'd even used deodorant this morning. Fortunately, that wasn't his problem since he wasn't Davis's supervisor.

Davis shut his door and instantly all eyes had shifted in their direction. The camera's started flashing, hands started raising among the sea of hungry reporters clamoring for a statement on what was shaping up to be the hottest case of the decade. Corder knew when he got the call to come in that morning for a special detail that it was going to be a media circus. Didn't mean he had to like it. Information had leaked that after all these years she finally wanted to talk. The reason was currently shrouded in mystery.

Silence had been her bedmate from the time of her arrest until today. Corder was beyond curious as to why she had chosen now to come forward. Every detective currently still on active duty had meticulously studied the details of the case. Perhaps the isolation had eaten away at her psyche and she couldn't bear it anymore, Corder wondered? No possibilities were being ruled out until they could talk with her face to face.

"I'll part the seas," Davis said without taking his eyes off the hoard of reporters as he took point. He loudly cleared his throat and his deep baritone voice called out for them to make a path.

Questions bombarded them from all sides, camera flashes temporarily blinded them, and microphones were thrust into their faces asking for statements, new information, etc. Stone faced, the two pushed their way forward into the building without too much heckling from the vultures.

"The Collier County Sheriff's Office has no comment at this time. Any new information will be shared when deemed appropriate" Corder said as they entered the building.

Thankfully, the circus wasn't allowed into the lobby and after a few seconds to breathe, they backed away from the doors. Both detectives put their issued weapons in the lock box and proceeded to the door to be buzzed in by Controls. The door opened as a corrections officer nodded to them. Once inside, they were escorted down to one of the visitation rooms.

The warden stood outside, hands clasped in front of him, shuffling from one foot to the other. A charcoal gray suit, faded at the edges, and creased on the shoulders, an off-white tie against a cream shirt was the biggest clue to this man's identity. Topping off the ensemble was the shiny nameplate affixed to his breast that displayed 'Warden'. He had stopped them prior to entering with a gesture of his hand. The scent of his cologne was strong enough to do that on its own and not in a good way. Pine needles and stale cheese... one of those may have been coming from him though. Both detectives could hear him breathing a good twenty feet from him.

"She wouldn't give us any information other than that she wanted to shed some new light on the case. Just a week ago she was all but comatose, was even wearing a diaper for fuck's sake. She's a nut job if you ask me. Whole family was," he said, handing over a thick folder.

Corder assumed the documents inside were from the case. Pictures of the suspects, victims, location of the murders...

"We're familiar with the case Warden but thank you," Corder said with a knowing smile, declining to take the folder.

"Sorry, you misunderstand Detective. This is just the file on her since she's been with us. Psych evaluations, incidents, uses of force, and what not."

Davis nodded, taking the folder from the warden and looked into the room at the woman seated at a table inside. She calmly stared back, with a slight smile. Her pale complexion and unkempt hair were clearly products of her environment. Nothing about her gave any credibility to what the Warden had told them. "We appreciate it. Anything we need to know before we walk in there?"

The woman sat with her hands folded on the table in front of her, dark, wavy hair dropping to just below her shoulders, inquiring green eyes locked onto the men outside the door. The red uniform the facility issued to all the inmates did nothing to complement her figure, but her attractiveness was undeniable. Her eyes conveyed a startling intelligence and clarity far beyond what her image was portraying.

"Don't underestimate her. It's easy to forget that she aided in the murder of at least twenty people. Maybe more. Not sure if we'll ever really know the full extent of the atrocities her family committed."

Without another word, the Warden shook their hands and headed off to another part of the compound.

A slow half smile crept across her face as the two detectives entered the room, hoping to uncover some new truths about one of the most gruesome killing sprees ever to occur in Florida's history. Her green eyes took on a predatory look, the features on her face was one of a lioness assessing her prey, and it sent shivers up Corder's spine. Goosebumps broke out on Davis's skin.

CHAPTER 1

August 5th, 1987

Summer had arrived in all her glory and was holding nothing back. The heat was stifling and the humidity suffocating. Outside activities were regularly accompanied by sweat, mosquitos and the sweet smell of barbecue. None but the natives of Florida would stomach this type of heat and they did so sweating with pride. At night the temperature dropped slightly, which made going out at night the pleasurable and sensible thing to do, depending on where you resided.

There weren't many residential areas in the vicinity of Florida's Alligator Alley but those that lived there would advise you not to venture out at night, for obvious reasons. The buzz of mosquitos and calls of other nightly insects and animals were a common and expected ritual of the 'Glades. The crunch of grass under heavy boots was a new sound to the nightly orchestra. However, recently it was more of a regular occurrence in this particular area and so was the increase in alligator activity.

The two men walking along the bank of the water were of similar build and height, age is what separated them. Both wore black, heavy raincoats with the hoods pulled down. Snake proof boots, thick wool socks, and blue jeans weren't optional in this swampy area. One carried a flashlight, keeping the darkness at bay and an eye out for any curious reptiles that happened to wander into their path. On his belt were a seven-inch bowie knife and a .38 revolver. The other was hefting two large black trash bags over his shoulder. His breathing got heavier and louder the farther they walked. The load he was carrying, that he had boasted in the beginning was a breeze, now was slowly wearing him down.

The flashlight cut a path back and forth in front of them and at times behind. Didn't want anything to come at them from the rear and catching them unaware. Rustling in the bushes to their right was illuminated by the flashlight but dismissed by the father and son pair as a small rodent-like animal scampered away, scared by the harsh light. A collected sigh escaped them both as they continued their trek.

The fence was directly ahead, perhaps twenty yards away. Their dumping point. A three-foot section of the fence was cut, allowing access to the water that was just past the protection of the fence. Three months prior, they had severed the links upon discovering this perfect location due to the heavy traffic of alligators and other predatory animals that prowled the 'Glades. This time of night, no other soul was around.

"Why am I always the one who gets stuck hauling the bags?" The younger man drawled.

He dropped the bags from his shoulder and let them fall to the ground with a squishing sound. The beam of the flashlight held still and the older man, Jameson, looked over his shoulder in contempt.

"Do we have to have the same discussion each and every time we do this son? Stop your bitching. We're almost done. And for Christ's sake, don't drop the bags like that. We don't want them bursting like they did last month"

With a grunt of acknowledgement, Gabe hauled the bags back on his wide shoulders, resuming his chore of carrying the discarded remains and kept his mouth shut. He didn't need another lesson in what happened when his dad was pushed too hard about any certain subject. A light bruise around his right eye and cheek were reminder enough. Rotating his jaw hurt his upper right cheek something fierce. Fractured was what Gabe assumed since it still hurt to touch it even lightly.

Something was moving in the water by the time they reached the fence, and Jameson kept alert for any red eyes in the reflection of his flashlight beam. They'd yet to have an incident but the day they threw caution to the wind would be the day they became gator bait. Holding open the fence, Jameson motioned for his son to toss the bags through. Before throwing them, Gabe stabbed holes in them. A copper scent reached Gabe's nose as the pooled liquid began seeping out of the punctures.

The activity in the water immediately increased and Jameson nudged Gabe with his boot.

"Hurry up, or they're gonna come right up to the damn fence."

Nodding fervently, he heaved the bags through, and they landed with a splash in the water. Within seconds the agitation in the water turned into a feeding frenzy as three adult alligators tore through the bags and began consuming what was inside.

The pair watched in silence as the reptiles enjoyed their free meal. Jameson knew it would do no good if some of the bigger pieces were left intact.

Jameson checked that the fence had fallen back into place, and they headed back in the direction they'd come.

***

CHAPTER 2

7 days later

The lights were intensely bright and hot. The sweat was pouring off him in streams. The open black leather jacket, with red flames on the sleeves was like wearing his own personal, portable furnace. His black leather pants clung to him in all the worst places. All of that shit he could normally ignore because of the roar from his audience, especially when he was fueled by adrenaline and pregame rituals. This combination allowed him to forget about anything and everything else. That and the large quantities of booze and drugs currently flowing through his system aided in the hazy blanket he'd put over his mind.

With one foot on the monitor, he took a deep breath, closed his eyes, and launched into the opening lines of their most requested song, 'The Devil's Tears'. At twenty-three, Dylan Masterson was living out his childhood dreams of being a rock star. As lead singer of Forbidden Fruit, a band that some would argue was poised to become a major player in the Rock scene, he was given access to anything. Girls, drugs, booze. Two albums with over 300,000 copies sold, a fourteen-city tour, and recording a third album upon completion of the tour were a clear indication of their rise.

Tonight's show was another sellout. A thick fog of smoke hung in the air, three hundred and fifty people jammed uncomfortably into the location, and Dylan couldn't help but smile. Three years ago, they were going nowhere fast, playing gigs at rundown dives and bars, for embarrassing payouts: bar tabs and food. These were the types of places that one might want to consider getting a tetanus shot afterwards if they'd stepped into the bathroom. In those places, they'd be lucky if eight people were paying them any mind. They struck gold when a manager for a respected record company happened to stumble upon one of their demos, giving them the opportunity of a lifetime. They were rising above the imitators, wannabes and fakes that plagued the underground scene.

Fists pumped in the air, and voices lifted from the crowd as he ended the chorus. On stage, the four of them gave one hell of a performance and seemed like the closest of friends. Dylan strode over to Jerry, lead guitarist, and they posed back-to-back. Jerry's fingers moved in a blur as he began his solo and Dylan let out one of the screams that he was becoming known for.

Behind the scenes, trouble was brewing amongst the members. There was no denying that Dylan was an inconsiderate prick to his other band mates. At the end of the previous show, Dylan had needed help walking off the stage. His drinking was becoming more than excessive and several times he couldn't even make it through an entire show. The other band members were beginning to worry that the next recording session would have to be put on hiatus or worse. Dylan didn't realize the view the other members had of him was so low, or maybe he would have tried to correct his current descent into oblivion. On the other hand, ever since gaining something of a following, his care and passion seemed to be only for where he could get his next fix or buzz. Dylan was riding high on the rising popularity, both figuratively and literally.

Desirable, fit, muscular... those were some of the words

most women and some men would have used in conversation when describing Dylan four months ago. His weight had plummeted from one hundred and ninety-five pounds to one hundred and sixty in a short amount of time. But his voice remained a solid powerhouse.

As the song came to its end, Dylan motioned for the bartender to bring him another bottle. Six songs into the night and he was preparing to delve into his second bottle of the house whiskey. Stumbling slightly before righting himself, he raised his fist in the air as he ambled to the side of the stage to finish off the first bottle in one long gulp.

Jerry glanced over to Rob, the drummer, and shook his head. It would be a miracle if they could finish all fourteen songs before Dylan reached the point of no return. Rob nodded his head in understanding and glared towards their front man as he dropped the empty bottle and trod his way back to the microphone.

* * *

His eyes burst open as a powerful urge to vomit overwhelmed his senses and brought him out of his drunken coma. Falling out of the bed, he scrambled to the bathroom in a mess of sheets, barely making it before decorating the toilet with partially digested alcohol. Spasms racked his abdomen as he tumbled to the side on the tile floor and saw that his room was empty of any other occupants. Where the hell was he? His thoughts were a jumbled mess of incoherent images and snatches of conversations from the night before. A more vivid one reared its ugly head and he moaned.

Halfway through the tenth song, *Weight of the World,* he'd taken an unplanned walk off the front of the stage, ten feet to the lacquered wood floor. No one in the audience was prepared, nor were the bouncers, so his body and face got intimate with the floor. Pulling himself up on the side of the bathroom sink, he was almost afraid to see the face that stared back at him from the mirror.

Not too bad, all things considered. A light bruise on his left cheek, that was sure to get worse, slight swelling of his lip, and his sides hurt. That last one could be from evacuating the contents of his stomach three times in the past few hours. He was grateful that none of his teeth wiggled when he tested them with his tongue, but he did taste blood. He spat a bright red glob into the sink, wiped his mouth on the towel and slowly went back into the room to sit on the edge of the bed.

Still out of it, he made a line on the edge of the table next to the bed and snorted. He needed to get his head straight.

Head in his hands, he begged for everything to stop spinning and inhaled deeply as the drug made its way into his system. A slip of paper next to his bed caught his attention.

'Band meeting downstairs, 2:00 pm. If you're not there, we're leaving without you.'

The clock on the bedside table read 1:40.

"Shit!" he uttered, as he struggled to pull his jeans on and a random, wrinkled shirt from the floor. He didn't even bother with shoes.

CHAPTER 3

"We deal with this same bullshit every time and I'm sick of it!"

Rob tossed his fork down next to his place, appetite ruined even with the delicious mixture of food that covered his plate. A mix of macaroni and cheese, medium rare steak, garlic mashed potatoes, two rolls, and green beans. A cold beer completed his meal. Drinking was one thing; getting so hammered that you couldn't function was another.

"I know Rob, we all are. That's why we have to be honest and tell him straight up how it is. No more going easy on him," Jerry said, moving the food around on his plate also, having eaten most of it.

Gary walked over with a plate of biscuits and gravy, next to chicken fried steak. The hotel they stayed in had a decent restaurant next to the lobby and they were taking advantage of it. As he sat down, Dylan bolted around the corner, nearly knocking over an older woman who yelped at the sight of him.

Hair disheveled, wrinkled clothes that smelled of booze and cigarette smoke, bruise on his cheek... he was quite the sight. And he had no shoes on. He more closely resembled a homeless man than a hung-over rock singer.

"Over here," Rob put up his hand and motioned him over.

Apologizing to the woman, he quickly walked over and sat down next to Gary, whose eyes widened within a few seconds.

"Damn bro, you gotta take a fucking shower. You reek," he complained, spraying the table with crumbs and scooting his chair away.

Dylan gave him the bird, accompanied with a weak smile.

"How much do you remember of last night?" Rob's tone and face were serious.

In the back of his mind, part of Dylan knew this conversation was bound to come up again and he shrugged his shoulders.

"Enough to know that I fucked up royally. I'm sorry guys, really," he looked at each one in turn. "I swear on my life, no more drinking during shows. I'll get my act together!"

The other three exchanged glances that spoke volumes of their doubt. This was probably the fifth, maybe sixth time that they had heard this same promise presented with the sad, pleading eyes. The problem was it was an empty promise that carried no weight.

"Look, Dylan, we've known each other for going on six years. I love you like a brother, but your promises just don't mean shit anymore. The last four shows we weren't even able to finish out the set. That leads to disappointed, angry fans which then turns into low record sales because we can't live up to their expectations. I am not okay with that man. Our fans deserve an excellent show, and we deserve a front man that we can count on."

As Rob was talking, Dylan's eyes roved back and forth among them, seeking, but not finding, any sympathy. The smell of the food on the table brought up conflicting pangs of hunger coupled with a wave of nausea that made his mouth water.

"This third album has the potential to raise us to new

heights and really put us on the map. Don't you want to play sold out shows with thousands of screaming fans chanting our names?"

Dylan nodded slowly but words failed him. His tongue was thick and dry. Swallowing painfully, he croaked, "You know I do."

Jerry leaned forward intensely, "Then prove it!"

Digging into his biscuits smothered in gravy, Gary said, "You're one talented son of a bitch, but you've got to slow down and take it easy on the partying and drinking side. We're all for having a kick ass time, but you have to know your limits."

Dylan put his hands on the table in front of him and took a breath. Previously, he would nod his head and just agree before sweeping it under the rug and forgetting about it. Their faces and tones of voice did not allow for that this time. They were seriously considering letting him go if he didn't shape up. He motioned at the cup of ice water on the table and Rob nodded. Taking a drink, he gathered his thoughts before speaking.

"Give me one last chance. Please! We have another show tonight in Miami. I'm sober now and will not have a drop of alcohol at the show, I swear on my mother's life. If I mess this up in any way, I'll leave the band, end of story and peacefully. You have my word," Dylan said, putting his hand out towards the center of the table.

After a few painful seconds of waiting on Dylan's part, Rob placed his on top, and the other three soon followed. This would be turning over a new leaf for Dylan. The show in Tampa had ended in disappointment and shame... Miami was going to be blown away by their performance. He just sensed that something big was on the horizon.

***

CHAPTER 4

The engine purred to life as Dylan prepared to leave the hotel and start the final leg of their tour. Following a hot shower and shave, he felt remarkably clear. Mentally at least, but physically he felt as if a bus had run him down, then reversed back over him. He considered himself more than lucky that the guys hadn't pulled the plug on everything back in the restaurant. Dylan racked his brain, trying to remember when he'd last performed a show completely sober... no memories came to him. Maybe he did have a problem.

Shaking his head brought on a sharp spike of pain in his head. Leaning his head back against the head rest, a conversation poked its head out of the fog he once called his memory. From his pocket came a joint he'd stashed away at some point last night.

"I know how you are Dylan. I'm so happy for you and the band but be careful."

Natalie, Dylan's sister, was four years older and knew him better than anyone else could claim. Since he was fifteen, he'd been sneaking liquor and beer from their father's stash. She was concerned about what being on the open road, the freedom to do whatever, and alcohol being handed to him on a daily basis, free of charge, would do to him.

"Come on Natalie. I'm not that bad, and I know my limits. Don't worry, everything's gonna be great. You'll see when we get back."

The look on Natalie's face betrayed the words that she desperately wanted to say but she shut the door on them. It wouldn't do any good and would probably piss him off.

"Just be safe okay. Have fun but please promise me you'll be safe."

Blinking his eyes rapidly as tears began to appear, he sat up and punched it, trying to escape the last conversation he'd had with his sister and image of her face that was forever seared into his mind. It didn't work. It was like a switch had been flipped in his head, allowing thoughts he'd try to keep buried, to burst free like an infected abscess and run rampant through him. With the flick of his lighter, Dylan took a long drag before tossing the joint out the window.

On their sixth stop, in Jacksonville, he'd received news from his mother that his sister had been killed in an armed robbery at a gas station, four miles from her apartment. Wrong place at the wrong time. She had been getting gas, and some snacks for the road; she was preparing to come and see him at his next show. As she was in line to pay, the man had approached unnoticed from behind. Gun digging into her back, he'd made her empty her purse. The cash and credit cards she carried went into the pocket of his coat. Without explanation or reason, he shot her twice in the back before killing the cashier and emptying the till.

The speedometer approached eighty-five miles an hour as he sped along the highway, weaving his way around the drivers obeying the speed limit, who blared their horns at him in response.

The police had no leads due to the man concealing his face behind a black mask, wearing heavy dark clothing and gloves to keep his identity secret. That night had been the first of the shows he didn't finish. He didn't have the strength to tell the other band members and told himself that he could handle this on his own. How wrong that had turned out to be.

The drugs and alcohol were the only ways that helped to keep his anger and sadness sedated. He opened his glove box and withdrew the bottle of Johnnie Walker he'd put there sometime the previous day. Battling with himself, he put the bottle in the seat next to him. The lead singer the band needed and deserved was long gone and had died that day in Jacksonville. He'd become quite successful at putting on a mask and pretending to be someone he just wasn't anymore.

"Fuck it," he muttered, and took hold of the bottle.

* * *

They walked past Dylan's black Mustang and Jerry kicked one of the tires. Strolling over to their van, which had Forbidden Fruit on the side in crooked letters, they piled in and headed off to Miami. He'd purchased the car right before the tour and insisted on driving it. This trip had driven a solid wedge between Dylan and the other members of the band. It wasn't worth the argument or time, so they didn't voice their opinions.

With the instruments and equipment in the van, it limited them in terms of the speed they would travel. The drive to Miami was about four hours, depending on traffic, but depending on how long Dylan took, they could end up getting there a hell of a lot sooner.

"Do you think he means what he says this time?" Gary inquired from behind the wheel, breaking the tense silence.

Jerry just shook his head, not willing to give an answer.

"Who really knows? If he doesn't, then we look at our options and move forward. I hope for his sake that he does. It'll be a step in the right direction if we get set up and he's not sitting at the bar nursing a drink."

* * *

CHAPTER 5

Leaning against the side of the truck, he stared aimlessly at the stars above him, daydreaming. His mind was constantly wandering among random things that caught his attention. The smile that began to appear on his face quickly transformed into a grimace of pain. Rubbing his jaw, he brought his full focus back to the task at hand. The pain in his jaw had lessened but still served as a reminder to keep him attentive. He didn't relish another "lesson" from his father.

Discipline was the one aspect of parenthood that he claimed to have mastered. Not even close to the word that Gabe would have used. Discipline was supposed to be instilled with love and used for the purpose of redirecting behavior. Abuse was the appropriate term for what Jameson offered up as correction.

Gabe was just relieved and happy that Jameson allowed him to be out unsupervised. Maybe he was gaining some favor in his dad's eyes. The stars sparkled above him as he counted them and made unrealistic wishes on them while keeping an ear out for the unmistakable sound of an approaching vehicle.

The improvised spike strip he'd fashioned was draped across the highway, waiting to deliver to him his next customer. Using the tools his father kept in the old shed and bits of metal, glass, and thick nails, he had created his own unique version that worked surprisingly well. There was that one incident, near the beginning, where his contraption had failed miserably, enacting quite the pounding from his father. Bed bound for a few days.

At twenty-eight, Gabe didn't know anything other than working for his parents at their restaurant. His job was simple: to provide the meat. He'd watched his father round up hitchhikers and the like, but as of late, hitchhiking was going out of fashion. Gabe was proud of the fact that the current method they employed was his brainchild, his baby.

It was one of the few times his father had said the four words he yearned to hear: I'm proud of you.

The only time to put the strip to use and avoid any unwanted attention or notice was at night. Less traffic meant the chances of being spotted were significantly lower. Gabe had no trouble subduing travelers. At six feet, three inches and two hundred and thirty-five pounds... he could hold his own. The gender of the unfortunate person made little or no difference, but he did tend to hope that the person was of a huskier stature. They were able to get more out of them. And the added bonus of releasing any pent-up aggression was always nice, and there was never a short supply of that.

No headlights approaching in either direction. Crossing his legs, he averted his eyes to the stars once more, listening to the engine of his truck tick as it cooled down. It was tucked away off the side of the road so that drivers coming from either direction wouldn't notice it. Gazing at the twinkling stars, a memory from years before crawled its way to the surface of his mind.

* * *

"Do you think you can handle it by yourself Gabe?"

His father was entrusting the important task of finding their supply of meat to him. The norm was for him to accompany his father, observe him, and do the heavy lifting.

Gabe nodded his head eagerly and couldn't help but be thrilled at the chance to prove himself to Jameson, who expected nothing less than perfection from his family. His mother's smile boosted his confidence and reassured him.

"Well, get to it then."

Gabe had roughly three hours to find someone and bring them back to the restaurant. They opened at ten and it wouldn't do well for business to have screams coming from the back room. *No need to worry Mr. Thomas. That's just your entrée refusing to cooperate. Would you care to sample some wine?*

It didn't take too long to find either a hitchhiker or someone broken down on the Alley. It wasn't a question of if but more so of when. Due to the lessons high school provided, Gabe had become a master at wearing masks. Having practiced smiling in the mirror long enough... eventually it became an involuntary function such as breathing. Sometimes he had trouble separating himself from the image he projected and his actual identity.

The headlights of the truck captured a figure walking along the shoulder with a bag over one shoulder. Gabe pulled up next to them and rolled the window down. The figure turned towards him, and he nearly swallowed his tongue.

She was undeniably beautiful. Sparkling green eyes, shoulder length chestnut brown hair, light tan face. She was wearing a dark blue tank top, and a black skirt that ended a couple of inches above her knees. The words he wanted to say wouldn't come. A small part of him urged him to roar off into the night, leaving her behind. There would be someone else.

"Are you going to offer me a ride or just sit there staring at me?"

Even her voice was lovely.

"Sorry. Yes, of course."

She tossed the bag into the bed of the truck and eased herself into the truck. Now he was fucked. How could he tell her to get out of the car and not look like an asshole? He was at war with himself and picturing his dad's angry visage did wonders for narrowing down his options. She maneuvered herself in the seat, getting comfortable before offering her hand.

"I'm Megan."

"Gabe," he responded after a slight pause. "Where are you headed?"

"Anywhere. Been on my own for a couple months now. I just had to get away from my parents and all of their rules and constant nagging," she said, staring out the window. "Do you get along with your family?"

Gabe shrugged his shoulders. "As much as any normal person I guess."

She snorted and Gabe cringed inwardly. *Really, even her snorts are cute.*

"Compared to mine, I bet your parents would win the parents of the year prize."

Gabe grunted in response. She would find out soon enough what kind of parents he had and there was no doubt she would change that statement. Sweaty palms, dry mouth, nervous grunts Gabe was surprised at how quickly this woman was turning him into a basket case. They were just two miles from the turnoff, and he felt as if he was being pulled apart on the inside. Two sides of him were battling it out over his next decision. The side that wanted to please his father dealt the winning blow.

He slowed the truck and pulled to the side of the road.

24

The confusion on her face was evident but he acted before she could voice any concern.

"I'm sorry."

His hands were around her throat and squeezing within seconds. Watching his father do this very task numerous times afforded him the knowledge of where to apply pressure without killing someone. From her angle she couldn't put up much of a fight. She squirmed, kicked her feet out in front of her, hitting the glove box a few times to no avail. Eyes bulging with fear, she scratched at his arms, drawing rivulets of blood which only made him increase the pressure. Her strength ebbed as she began to lose consciousness and he carefully removed his hands. A tear dropped onto his cheek, and he hurriedly wiped it away before checking for a pulse. Slow, but there. His arms burned and there were four lines on each arm where she'd hoped to stop him.

The look on his father's face when he handed over his prize was almost worth it. Almost. No "Good job Gabe" or anything like that. Gabe could count on one hand how many times his father had smiled because of something he'd done.

Her head moved slightly as he watched her from across the room. *Please don't wake up until I'm out of the room. Please! Please!* A moan from her throat signaled her return from dreamland. Silently, he backed up and crept to the door.

A soft but scratchy voice called to him. "What's going on?"

He could hear his father and mother talking in the other room. His sister was probably asleep in her room. She never had to do any of the hard work. Daddy's little girl was allowed to get her precious sleep.

"I'm sorry." he whispered.

Her memory came flooding back and she looked at him with apprehension, anger, fear, and confusion.

"Just let me go. Please. I won't tell anyone. I don't even know who you are."

She continued to plead her case. To his astonishment, his weaker side started to listen and rationalize it. Who would she tell? He could say she escaped and then find someone else to take her place. One moment of compassion led to him having a kind of outer body experience.

He watched, bewildered, as his hands undid the rope and his voice whispered, "Don't say a word. Go out the door to your left. Stay away from the woods. Get to the road and just keep going."

What the hell was happening? A small part of him was relishing this moment and felt good, while the other part was experiencing a mixture of shock and curious fascination.

She stood and hugged him tightly. Her scent was still intoxicating and paralyzing simultaneously. Hands shaking, he hugged her back and felt her embrace tighten around his neck and her body moved even closer which he didn't think was possible. She rubbed her cheek against his before pulling away slightly and kissed him on the cheek then whispered in his ear, "Thank you!"

He found himself standing alone in the storeroom, watching her close the door quietly behind her before seeing her shadow streak off towards the road. A commotion from the direction Megan had run distracted him from his thoughts, and he rushed outside.

Elena was standing over Megan, who lay sprawled among the trash cans. Her yellow sundress stopped just short of her knees, dark hair hung loosely about her shoulders, and her smile was captivating. His sister's beauty was the perfect disguise for the sinister nature and desires that lay hidden just under the surface. From what Gabe could tell, Megan had come around the corner at the same time as Elena and his sister had thrown or knocked her into them.

"Look what I found!"

The glee in her voice was unmistakable.

His father's voice echoed from inside.

"What the hell is going on out there?!"

Gabe lowered his head with a combination of anger, guilt, and embarrassment. He couldn't bear to look into Megan's eyes. His father stormed out and leveled his gaze, first at Elina, then at Megan, and finally settling on Gabe. Confusion shifted to realization as the situation sunk in. Jameson's gaze turned hard, well, harder as the veins in his neck started to pulsate to the beat of his growing anger. Elena had Megan's hair twisted in her hand, keeping her whimpering in place on her knees. If Megan attempted to move, Elena would give a sharp tug, eliciting a painful yelp from Megan. Seething, Jameson went back inside. His outline could be seen walking to the living quarters which were connected to the restaurant. Heavy breathing was the only sound as they waited.

Jameson returned with his shotgun in his hands.

"For a moment I was actually proud to call you my son. Elena, go inside with your mother. I need to talk to your brother alone."

Always the obedient one, she released Megan and smelled her hand. "I'm sorry we didn't have more time with each other," she said as she knelt in front of Megan. Closing her eyes, she put both hands on the side of Megan's face and kissed her gently on the forehead while Megan cried. With a satisfied nod, Elena stood up and skipped inside, humming to herself. Megan's eyes darted back and forth between Gabe and Jameson.

"Run."

Megan didn't move, not sure whether she'd heard Jameson right. His eyes were wild with fury, and he nodded his head once. She looked to Gabe for some sign of what to do but his head was still down. She stood up, gave one last look to Gabe, and then took off towards the road at an awkward run. She must have injured her leg when she fell.

Jameson roughly grabbed his son by his hair, pulling his head back so that he could see Megan.

"I want you to remember this the next time you decide to defy me," he said, raising his shotgun to his shoulder.

* * *

CHAPTER 6

Windows down, hair blowing in the warm breeze, Dylan sped down the alley. According to the directions, he was about two hours away from the club. Occasionally the Mustang would veer to one side or the other but he quickly corrected it. Opening the glove compartment to check for a second bottle frustrated him. *One bottle will have to do.*

He tossed the empty bottle to the back seat and directed his attention back to the road. It had been at least half an hour since he'd passed another car but coming up on his right was the third animal he'd passed. Roadkill was a common sight on the alley and a reminder to keep vigilant. Hitting an alligator or deer at his current speed would be fatal. His mood instantly brightened upon remembering that he had stashed a second bottle upon leaving the bar the previous night. Checking to make sure no one was coming the other way, he began foraging around in the center console. The first few seconds resulted in nothing as his hand brushed cassettes, food wrappers, something sticky that caused him to cringe at the thought of what it could be, but no bottle.

"What the hell?" he muttered, wiping his hand on the seat.

Searching for the mysterious, vanishing bottle, he failed to see the strange obstruction in front of him that stretched across the width of the road. The tires blew upon impact, throwing him forward and to the side. At eighty-seven miles an hour, he was lucky he didn't break his nose or worse.

Sparks flew as the metal grated noisily on the road. Not knowing what happened or really what to do, he struggled to regain control of the wheel but overcorrected. The car fishtailed left, and then spun to the right. As the ruined tires lost contact with the road, the car flipped, and time slowed to a crawl for Dylan. He had a moment to recollect that the second bottle was lying empty in the trash bin of his hotel room before his head connected with the roof and all went black.

* * *

CHAPTER 7

Young, a bit on the thinner side, minor head wound that wasn't life-threatening. Gabe was proud of his catch but now was sweating heavily as he threw the man over his shoulder and marched towards his truck. The bed of the truck was spacious and clear of any clutter. He placed the man in the back before covering his body with a tarp. He grabbed the can of gas and a set of matches for this next part.

"Looks like I fucked up your vehicle really good," he said to himself. "Damn lucky the crash didn't kill you. Pops would have had my head for that!"

He stopped before giving the car a healthy splash of gas. Something glinted from the interior, and he smiled at his luck: an empty liquor bottle. Peeking in through the side window that had shattered, he assessed the situation as best he could. Unable to find any remnants of alcohol on the seats, roof, or floor led him to believe this man had been drunk driving.

"That would explain the reckless driving," he said, nodding to himself as he decided not to douse the car and strode back to his truck. He wasn't the sharpest tool in the shed. The thought and issue of the missing body when someone eventually came across the accident scene failed to register any significance in his mind.

A light moaning issued from under the tarp. Gabe whistled as he hopped into the bed of the truck, looking upon the outline of the man under the tarp as it moved slowly. The squirming stopped as Gabe let loose with a few swift kicks to the general area he assumed was the man's stomach.

"I know you can hear me. If you so much as move a finger, or make a sound, I will gut you like a pig and dump your body in the water for the gators. You understand?"

A vigorous nodding from under the tarp brought a smile, and he kicked him once more for good measure and to make his point.

"I said no moving," Gabe said with a snicker. No movement this time. "Glad we understand one another."

Opening the passenger door, he withdrew a stained, wooden baseball bat. "My trust is the one thing you do not have," he whispered.

Humming, he skipped back to the end of the truck, twirling the bat in his hand. He swung the bat down with enough force to make sure the guy was down for the time being. No movement or noise. Gabe didn't want him waking up while in transport to the restaurant.

* * *

"This is ridiculous. I told you we shouldn't have let him drive himself." Gary said, leaning against the side of the van.

"Bullshit! You're the one who went all googly eyed over the new ride like a high school girl picking out her prom dress," Jerry said from his position sitting on the ground to the side of the club entrance. "How much longer do we wait before we cancel the gig?"

They were supposed to be on stage, opening with the first song, in thirty minutes and Dylan was a no show. Cancelling a show never looked good and reflected badly on the band. It meant refunds, pissed off fans, and taking a venue off the list of places to perform at in the future. A no show brought about a resolute 'fuck you' from the owner and a bashing of your name to every person they knew.

Rob didn't understand it. This wasn't typical behavior of Dylan. Getting obnoxiously drunk during a performance was one thing, not showing up was a different animal altogether.

"He's never flaked on a gig before guys," Rob said with concern. "I hope nothing happened to him."

"You know he's probably shacked up at some bar around here, throwing them back as usual."

The doors to the club burst open, releasing a cloud of smoke mixed with the noise of a packed house. Framed in the smoke was a portly looking man. Seeing the band, the owner hurried over, his stomach drooping over his belt from one too many beers. Dark purple dress shirt, top two buttons open giving a glimpse of a gold chain nestled in his chest hair, started off the laughable ensemble. Topping it all off was a pair of tight black pants, and sunglasses hanging from his collar. His face was flushed with what one could naturally assume was anger.

Jerry stifled a laugh and turned his head to the ground as Gary whispered to Rob, "He's all yours bud!"

* * *

CHAPTER 8

It felt like his head was splitting in half. Dylan wasn't stupid and heard his assailant whisper to himself before taking a deep breath. The bat glanced his head and met the floor of the bed. That's the only reason he was still conscious. Had it been slightly higher...

It took every ounce of his will power to stay quiet and not react to the pain radiating from the cheap shot. Fortunately, it was only a few seconds before the truck's engine roared to life and they were moving. Rolling his neck carefully from side to side hurt but he had range of motion. It would be tender for some time but he would live. Every bump sent new waves of pain through his body. The chance for escape would come and he would pounce on it. His fingers found the bat that the guy had dropped next to him.

That was a mistake Dylan would make sure he paid for in full. The hardest part about being in the back of the truck and playing as if he was unconscious was letting himself slide with the movements of the truck.

The truck turned slightly, pitching him into the side of the bed before it hit what could have been a ditch or small animal. This guy's driving skills left much to be desired. Biting down on his lip helped him stay quiet. He wasn't sure if the windows were down but that's the last thing he needed at the moment. Surprise was going to be in his favor, and he intended to take advantage of it. He hunkered down, preparing to launch his attack when the tarp was removed.

* * *

The truck slid to a stop, and he heard his cargo slam into the back of the cab.

"Hope that didn't hurt too much," he muttered to himself as he opened the door.

The squeaking was loud and on a frequency that would make dogs go berserk. Considering the condition of his pick-up, Gabe really shouldn't complain. The dark blue paint had become more of a pale misty color and was peeling in multiple places. The engine had started to issue an annoying clicking sound when the speedometer went over thirty. Probably a sign of trouble brewing, but fixing the truck wasn't at the top of Gabe's priority list.

"I got us one," he hollered, knowing one of his family members would hear him.

His mom was probably in the kitchen getting it prepped, his sister cleaning and setting up the dining area, and his dad... tucked away setting up his workspace. The storeroom was connected to the restaurant by a short hallway and held all of their food stuffs: flour, cooking oils, utensils, sugar, produce, etc. There was a large refrigerator that currently was stocked with chicken breasts, fresh fish, various vegetables and condiments, and two containers of meat from Gabe's last prize that would be used for appetizers. It wasn't enough to shake a stick at which was why he had to go out tonight. Once a week was normally enough but it just depended on the person's size, and how busy the restaurant was.

Steaks, and the Jameson special were popular items on the menu, so they had to keep the meat in stock. There were times where Gabe had moments of doubt about what they did but his father had a way of squashing them... quite forcefully.

A light came on in the storeroom, so Gabe turned his attention to unloading his cargo. The tarp got hooked on something near the front of the truck and it wouldn't budge. He hauled himself onto the bed of the truck to get better leverage and pulled again.

* * *

CHAPTER 9

The footsteps came around the bed of the truck on his right side and he wrapped his hand up in the edge of the tarp next to his face. The other held the bat firmly and he waited. The first tug wasn't hard. The following one nearly tore his arm out of the socket, but he leaned into it, easing the pressure. The truck sank down lower on the tires and Dylan knew the man was in the truck with him. Opening his hand freed the tarp and he took a two-handed grip on the bat, anxious to see the face of his captor.

The tarp flew off fast and he saw the man's balance falter. It's what he was counting on. Tucking his feet under him, he shot up and swung the bat upward with all the strength he could muster. Slipping on the tarp robbed some of the force and momentum away from the hit but it still did the trick. The man's head snapped back with a crack and his body tumbled backwards out of the truck.

He heard a door open from his right and didn't risk a glance in that direction. Head pounding and feeling slightly dizzy, he kept his hold on the bat and seized his chance for escape. Jumping over the left side of the truck, he pumped his legs and took off towards the safety of the woods. The distance was closing fast and he urged his body forward. The yell of anger and confusion from behind him only fueled his adrenaline and speed.

* * *

CHAPTER 10

Jameson's anger exploded out of him like a raging animal at the scene that greeted him upon opening the door of the storeroom. His son was on the ground, not moving, and a person was running at full speed for the woods. It wasn't hard to surmise what had led to the current predicament.

A moan from his son answered the question on whether or not he was dead. Not that he would be too terribly upset, would just mean an increased workload on himself. Approaching his son, he shook his head in disbelief at his failure. Sweat covered Gabe's face, and a line of blood and spit dripped from his torn lip.

The vague outline of the escape artist disappeared into the tree line. Face scrunched in pain, his son sat up and reached a hand to him. Jameson swatted it away with disgust.

"Worthless. You have one fucking job to do and you manage to fail at that. Now I've got to go clean up after your mess. What good are you to me if you can't carry your own weight?"

Turning his back on his son, he strode back to the storeroom without giving Gabe a chance to defend and explain himself. A few seconds later, Jameson emerged from inside, rifle in hand, and a determined look on his face. Gabe staggered to his feet, gingerly touching his jaw which ached something fierce. The guy had got quite the drop on him. He brushed off his hands on the side of his jeans and still had a bewildered expression on his face.

"Go inside and help the women. Do you think you can handle that?"

Gabe stood an inch or two taller than his father, but the man still intimidated him. The look of hurt on his face disappeared, replaced with one of hatred and violence. Jameson's back was to him as he trekked towards the woods.

"Asshole." Gabe couldn't believe the word had come from his mouth but a part of him was proud.

Jameson stopped and shot a glance over his shoulder.

"What did you just say?"

Gabe stood to his full height, puffed out his chest and repeated himself. Louder this time, "I called you an asshole."

Faster than Gabe expected, his father rushed him and hit him in the gut with the butt of the rifle. The air burst from him and he wavered on his feet, pleading with his body to stay upright. The last thing he wanted was to appear any weaker to this bastard who called himself a father. His knees buckled but he caught himself before falling on his face. Taking short breaths kept the pain to a minimum. He clenched his hand into the grass and into the dirt beneath it, knuckles turning white from the strain.

A scream exploded from the woods interrupting his father's current course of action. Gabe closed his eyes, allowed his hands to relax and thanked the stars for the reprieve.

"We're going to have a long talk later about your lack of respect when I get through fixing the problem that you created."

* * *

CHAPTER 11

Branches snatched at his clothing and scratched at his arms and face. The more distance he could put between himself and these people, the better off he would be. Even with his restricted vision, he didn't dare slow down. He avoided colliding with a tree at just the last second due to blind luck more than anything.

The direction didn't matter, as long as he continued to move at a steady clip. He was bound to come upon a place to seek help from.

A biting pain and twist from his right ankle brought him crashing to the ground. His adrenaline was soaring and he tried to get back to his feet but felt a searing pain in the lower part of his leg. Dylan's mind had trouble believing the images it was being sent.

The flesh of his leg above his ankle was flayed open to the bone and caught in what seemed to be a bear trap. Blood poured through his fingers as he frantically tried to pull at the teeth that were currently sunk into his leg. His fingers continued to slip due to the bloodied metal. The teeth moved apart an inch, then two before sliding through his bloodied fingers to close again. He screamed to the open sky as they scraped and ground on bone.

* * *

Jameson had strategically placed bear traps in a two-mile radius around the restaurant. Sometimes an unlucky animal or two got caught in them but that wasn't their intended purpose. This wasn't the first time a person had tried running from them and he was now fully prepared for any unforeseen circumstances.

It wasn't hard to determine the direction of the scream because the person was making a hell of a lot of noise. Not that he could blame him. The problem was that the more a person moved, the more damage was done by the device. The half-moon provided just enough light to see the young man sitting on the ground struggling with the bear trap. The ground around his leg was a dark crimson and his face was pale and sweaty due to the loss of blood. He was concentrating so hard on freeing himself that he had yet to notice Jameson's approach.

Without making a sound, he raised the rifle and sighted to the man's chest, then fired.

* * *

CHAPTER 12

Droplets of blood continued to leak from his nose like a dripping faucet, collecting on the floor in small puddles. Gabe sat forward in the chair, hoping to keep the blood off of his clothes, waiting for his mother to come in with a towel so he could try and staunch the flow. It wasn't his fault the guy took off running. He'd knocked him over the head with the bat prior to heading back home. *You should have double checked when you parked the truck. You're pathetic. Trust but verify. How many times do I have to tell you that!?*

He shook his head, ridding himself of his father's scornful voice that was sure to creep back in later and fester like an infected wound.

"Damn it," he said harshly, as a few drops of blood landed on his pants.

"Keep quiet Gabe," a woman's voice called softly from behind him. "Do you want your father coming back in here?"

He tilted his head and sighed as his mother walked in front of him offering him a warm towel. Pressing it to his nose, he leaned back and glared at the ceiling. Images of causing his father extreme amounts of pain were racing through his mind like a torture collage. His mother knelt in front of him and took his free hand in hers, caressing it lovingly as she looked up into his eyes.

"He does love you Gabe, regardless of what you might be thinking right now. He just has those moments where he lets his anger get the best of him. Mistakes happen and deep down he understands that," she said comfortingly, resting a hand against his cheek, wiping away a singular tear as it fell down Gabe's face.

She wore a vibrant yellow dress with a white apron over top. There were multiple red stains on the front of the apron. No matter what task she was performing, looking her best had always been a priority for her. Regardless of how chaotic or intense her life became she did not allow it to show and presented a beautiful façade that fooled just about anyone she encountered. It would be another couple of hours before they would be ready to open for customers. Prep time was hard, long work but also the most fun... for the Rifflet family.

"Eleanor, get in here. I need your help!"

"Coming dear," she answered, giving her son a loving smile and tender pat on his cheek before leaving the room.

Hearing his father's voice made Gabe grind his teeth. Jameson was harder on Gabe than he was on their daughter Elena, who was three years younger. In his mind she was his perfect little angel that could do no wrong. Gabe seemed to be nothing but a disappointment. Sniffing brought the taste of iron to the back of his throat and he spat it out on the ground instead of the alternative. He didn't harbor a taste for that sort of thing, unlike someone else he knew.

Movement to his right brought a slight smile to his face. It may not be his dad, but their newest addition would be the perfect outlet for all the rage and aggression that was boiling inside of him.

"Time to wake up my friend. You've rested long enough."

* * *

His thoughts were a tangled mess of images, sounds, and words that wouldn't come together to form anything coherent or useful. It felt like he was falling down a black hole with no hope of reaching the end. Voices called to him: his sister, his mom, Rob, Jerry, his ex-girlfriend Melissa, even his childhood friend Jimmy. Some were comforting while others were nagging and chastising all fighting for dominance over the others. The voices stopped as abruptly as they had begun. His eyelids fluttered as he regained consciousness. A voice spoke to him but he didn't recognize it. Frowning, he struggled to clear his vision and place the figure standing before him. The grogginess was taking longer to dissipate.

"Time to wake up my friend. You've rested long enough."

What the hell was happening? The last thing he remembered was...

Pain pulsed in his leg like a living thing, growing slightly more intense with each throb. Thinking was proving difficult as he rolled his tongue around in his mouth to try and generate enough saliva so he could speak.

"Where... what... happened?"

The blurry figure in front of him bent down and roughly checked the rope that kept his hands bound behind his back. Another thick rope had his legs tied firmly to the chair. No response from the man as he continued to check the ropes, cinching them a little bit tighter.

Dylan hummed to himself in pain and bit his lower lip. The pain was breaking up the fog that had invaded his brain. Parts of his memory returned but Dylan still couldn't make sense to how he had ended up in his current situation. He vaguely remembered racing through the woods before getting tangled in the bear trap then blackness, like there was a break in the film of his mind.

He was afraid to even chance a look at the damage to his leg but the need to know was overpowering. His vision shook slightly as he glanced down and saw that his leg was wrapped in gauze and bandaged. Someone had taken the time to treat his wound but it still ached, and he could see a little pink starting to come through the white of the dressings.

"The effects of the tranquilizer will wear off soon enough," the figure's voice broke through his pain addled mind, and with a jolt, he recognized the voice. The bastard who had kidnapped him.

The room's lighting came from two sources. One was a single bulb that hovered directly over Dylan's head and was swaying slightly, and the other was from a lamp to his right that sat on what looked like a crudely constructed work bench of some sort. Sitting on the bench was a silver tray containing a variety of surgical tools: a hack saw, scalpel, gauze, and other instruments that caused his heart to skip a beat or two. Hanging from the ceiling next to him were two massive gray hooks. He didn't want to dwell on what those were for. There were also four drains in the floor, spaced about two feet apart, in a square, nestled in the center of the room.

Dizziness settled in and he realized he'd been holding his breath while taking in his surroundings. Sweat trickled down his face as he tested the ropes on his arms and legs, hoping to find some wiggle room. His captor had made sure the ropes were tight but not to the point where they cut off circulation.

Sucking in a deep breath, he shouted, "SOMEBODY HELP ME! FOR GOD'S SAKE, SOMEONE…"

A filthy, stained rag shoved into his mouth cut off his screams. It went far enough in his mouth to activate his gag reflex. The gag tasted of sawdust, dirt, and God knew what else

"There will be none of that," the man said, backhanding him across his face.

Dylan's head rocked to the side and he spit the disgusting rag onto the floor in defiance before beginning his screams anew. The veins stood out in his neck as he yelled like a man with nothing left to lose. Neither one noticed the imposing shadow that was standing in the doorway to the room.

Gabe scrambled to put the rag back into his mouth and received a vicious bite on his hand for the trouble that drew blood.

"Fuck!"

Dylan's face scrunched in disgust at the taste enveloping his mouth: a tapestry of dirt, grease, sweat, and oil. Seeing his captor hold his hand close to his stomach in pain brought a small smile to his face though.

Jameson strode into the room, shoved his unhelpful son out of the way, grabbed Dylan by the back of his head, and brought his eyes up to his. Dylan's protests were stopped by the feel of something sharp and metallic against his tongue.

"If you say another word, I will cut out your tongue and feed it to the stray dogs out back, while you watch."

Shifting his eyes down gave him a sickening view of a long blade resting in the corner of his mouth. The hand was steady and didn't have even the slightest tremor.

"Nod once if you understand."

Dylan did so carefully so he wouldn't cut himself. Jameson smiled briefly, glanced in annoyance at his son, and put the blade away on his person. Cradling his injured hand, Gabe waited until Jameson left the room to get up and glare daggers at Dylan.

Leaning down so his face was level with Dylan's, he promised, "Better make your peace with your Maker because you're in for one hell of a ride."

Dylan wasn't one to give up without a fight, so he winked at his abductor just to piss him off and show that he wasn't going to play the part of the submissive, wounded prey. Gabe roughly shoved the rag back into his mouth and used duct tape to ensure that it stayed in place this time, wrapping it around Dylan's head three times.

* * *

CHAPTER 13

The night was dragging on as it usually did on night shift and the two men were battling sleep, doing whatever they could to keep awake: cards, discussing plans for the future, talking about what was happening in the precinct, etc. Both officers had been on the force for a little over three years and the night shift was where they had been assigned to post-academy. Positions on day shift rarely opened, and both spoken of going the route of specialty positions or promotions so transferring to dayshift was currently a moot point.

Mac popped a new stick of gum in his mouth, his fourth piece, and shifted in his seat, keeping his cards hidden. Nicorette didn't have much in the way of flavor, but it filled the void that cigarettes had occupied.

"Are you going for detective next month or are you going to come up with another excuse as for why you shouldn't?"

Looking up from his cards, Warren gave a fake smile, "There is a big difference between an excuse and a reason."

"Oh come off it. You know what I mean."

Mac was twenty-five, single, and had no family in Florida. He'd removed himself from an abusive household and had never looked back. Stopping abuse of all kinds was the main motivation to why he chose the career path of an officer. Passing him on the street, one would never correctly guess his profession. Five seven, slightly overweight, with a patchy mustache didn't quite grant him the label of an intimidating man of the law. Pizza delivery driver would possibly fit more one of his stature and demeanor.

Warren was the polar opposite. Twenty-seven, married, with his first child to be born in three months, he was the quintessential family man. Devoted to his family first, the job second. People avoided eye contact with him because he did have the intense stare and muscular build that commanded respect. Recently his mother had fallen deathly ill, and his father couldn't do it on his own, so he did all he could to help with her. He was lucky if he got four hours of sleep a day, but you would never hear a word of complaint come from his mouth.

Mac knew of the family issues Warren was facing but didn't really know how to respond to the situation, so he resorted to cracking jokes or playing dumb to it. It wasn't that he didn't care. He just had no experience in the area and Warren didn't hold it against him.

"So, you didn't really answer the question…"

Warren was grateful when the radio crackled to life, saving him from having to get into this conversation again.

"Dispatch to Unit 7, we've got a call for a possible missing person driving a black mustang, license plate Alpha Tango Four Charlie Two Six, last seen heading down I-75 South to Miami. Never made it to destination. Name's Dylan Masterson. Alcohol may be involved."

"Ten-four dispatch, Unit 7 on it," Mac answered.

Their car was pulled to the side of the road and hadn't seen a car in the last hour. Warren buckled his seat belt and nodded to Mac.

"Let's head north. I would have remembered seeing a Mustang pass us. Keep an eye out for headlights or taillights, car debris, anything that could give us a sign of an accident. Let's hope we just find him pulled to the side of the road taking a piss or passed out."

"I'll put fifty on finding him unconscious in the driver seat," Mac said with a laugh.

Knowing how horrible car accident clean ups could be, Warren declined taking the bet as they pulled off down the road, hoping for once that Mac was right.

      * * *

No body. Shining his flashlight in the car revealed little to nothing and left him baffled at the whereabouts of the person who drove the car. Warren did find possible evidence as to the cause of the accident quick enough when the light reflected off of the empty liquor bottle. Further inspection led him to believe possible foul play was involved though. The tires were shredded, but from what?

Mac was still on the radio, checking in and informing dispatch that they'd found the vehicle but no visual of the person yet.

He bent down to get a closer view of the tires and something caught his attention. A piece of metal jutted crookedly out of the remains of the front driver's side tire. Pulling on a pair of gloves from his pocket, he squatted down to get a better view. Wiggling it back and forth, he removed a three-inch chunk of some type of metal. He held it in the palm of his hand and saw it was fashioned to a sharp point at the end with rough, jagged edges. Following the trajectory that the car was on proved easy enough with his flashlight and he made his way back towards the road, hoping to find some clue as to what this guy could have hit or run over.

Waving his beam back and forth across the road revealed nothing. Mac called out to him but he waved him off as he continued his search. Footsteps rang out on the street behind him. Fifty feet down the road and there was no sign of any type of obstruction or debris that could have ripped through his tires with such ease.

"What are you looking for?" Mac asked, slightly out of breath but trying to hide it.

Clicking off his flashlight, Warren turned back towards the abandoned vehicle. Things weren't adding up and falling into place like he preferred.

"I'm at a loss for what he hit because there is no sign of anything on the road as far as I can tell, but something fucked up his tires bad. There's the smell of alcohol and we did find an empty bottle of Johnnie Walker on the floorboard. But something just isn't adding up. The chances that all four tires burst simultaneously are astronomical," he said, holding up the rusted piece of metal for Mac to inspect. "I pulled this out of one of the tires on the car."

"What the hell is that?"

Mac beckoned with his bare hand, and Warren hesitated for a moment before dropping it into Mac's hand. He made his way back over to the Mustang stripping off his gloves, shaking his head at the carelessness on Mac's part. God only knew where that thing was from or what it had come in contact with.

"What do you think happened?"

"A missing person, no sign of where he went to... some blood on the dashboard of the car, probably from hitting his head when the car flipped. I don't know yet," Warren responded as he crouched next to the car, sweeping the ground with his flashlight. "But I'm not comfortable labeling this as a drunk wrecking his car. I'm leaning towards foul play. We just need some credible evidence to justify my suspicions."

Tilting his head to the side to get a better angle, Warren

motioned for Mac to join him. There were two divots in the ground next to the driver's side door. "A body just doesn't vanish into thin air."

* * *

CHAPTER 14

A voice calling softly broke through the haze.

It sounded like his grandmother's voice, assuring him that everything was going to be fine like she used to when he'd gotten hurt as a young boy. When he'd heard her voice as a child, he'd been convinced that all the wrong in the world could be made right. A light brush against his cheek brought a smile. The soothing voice continued to speak to him, but he couldn't understand it at first.

A pair of the most beautiful hazel eyes greeted him as he opened his own to see the angel that was in his presence. Not his mother but a woman in her early twenties, sitting on his lap, with a dazzling smile present on her face as she coaxed him to wake up. A cream-colored V-neck shirt bordering on see-through and a pair of black underwear was all she was wearing. *What the hell is going on?*

"You've been out for quite some time." She rested her arms on his shoulders and sighed contentedly.

His tongue felt like a piece of rough sandpaper and his mouth was dry. Answering this very attractive woman was out of the question. Had the entire ordeal been a dream? Could he be that lucky? He tried raising a hand to touch the woman in front of him to see if she was real and the hard reality of the situation came crashing back in on him like a rogue wave. Without warning, she ripped open his shirt and tilted her head as she took in his physique. Were this any other time and place his mind would be travelling down other avenues with this gorgeous woman within his reach.

Her eyes searched his body inquisitively as if it contained some hidden treasure buried beneath his skin.

"You called for your nanna a little bit ago. Were you dreaming of her?"

Until I woke to find that my life has become a fucking nightmare. There was only one door that he could see out of this room. The gravity of his situation weighed heavily on his mind and kept his attention away from the beautiful distraction that rested on his lap. Not being able to see behind him limited his options to the front and sides. No windows either. How the hell was he supposed to get to out of this place?

A searing, sharp pain in his lower left abdomen caused him to almost see stars as he twisted and tried desperately to retreat from it. That just made the woman smile all the more.

"Stop squirming. You don't want me hitting anything important, do you? I just need to make a small incision so we can have our base ingredient for the broth."

A strangled cry escaped his lips as she pulled the knife back out. Blood began to trickle from the three-inch incision into a pot she'd put under the cut.

"Don't make too much noise," she said teasingly, holding up the rag in front of his face.

"Fuck... you!" Dylan rasped through clenched teeth with all the defiance he could muster.

Her eyes took on a mischievous glint as she maneuvered herself on his lap so that she straddled him, bringing her face close to his. Balling up the rag, she put it back into his mouth, and then lightly smacked his cheek. He breathed in her perfume, lilacs and strawberries, and was having trouble concentrating on his predicament. For a brief moment, he'd considered ramming his face into hers but feared the reaction of the rest of the people he'd met. A scowl would have to suffice for now.

"You are so cute," she cooed, lightly trailing her hand down his face, stopping to rest against his chest. He couldn't help but cringe at her touch. What was wrong with these people? She hummed to herself as her fingers crawled their way down to his stomach. His flesh broke out in goosebumps and he couldn't help but shiver. The farther down her hand travelled, the closer she moved her body to his. Mere centimeters separated them, and she smiled seductively at him. There was no denying that she was stunning but the fact that she was clearly insane wasn't hard to forget, even when she was sitting on his lap.

Her smile widened as her fingers found his wound and pushed their way in. His eyes widened in pain and shock as he bit down viciously on the rag.

"We need this to be a little bigger to get more from it," she said as she widened his cut with her fingers. "Otherwise, it'll take all day and we don't have that kind of time."

She picked up the pot and held it directly under the now four inch slit in his side. Pushing down on his abdomen above the wound increased the stream of blood and his level of pain. His blood filled a third of the pot already and she still didn't seem satisfied. Resting her head against his chest she twirled her bloody fingers through his chest hair.

"Saturdays tend to be one of our busier days, so we have to make sure to have enough soup to last us," she purred as she continued to play with his hair.

Dylan's vision blurred and he shook his head trying to fight away the light headedness. Sitting up from his chest, she gave a little giggle. He watched in horrid fascination as she sucked his blood off of her fingers one at a time. Eyes closed; she made a sigh of delight at the taste.

"Elena, how many times have I told you not to play with the food?"

She made a frustrated sound at the tone in her father's voice and stood up from Dylan's lap. Upon seeing Jameson, Dylan started straining against the ropes again. The knife from earlier was back in his hand and tapping against the side of his face as he studied Dylan. He nodded to Elena, who with a frown on her face, left the room, visibly upset at being interrupted.

"Close the door behind you," Jameson said, never shifting his gaze.

With a wink at Dylan, the monster closed the door, locking him in the room with a psychopath.

* * *

CHAPTER 15

Elena stood with her back against the door for a few seconds until she heard the music start. The blood sloshed in the pot as she made her way carefully into the kitchen. The vegetables for the stew were laid out on the counter next to the stove waiting to be cut; all her favorites. Carrots, celery, onions, and tomatoes. It wouldn't take but a half hour to get the soup going, and at that point she would require the meat to add in. A scream from the storeroom was a sure sign that she wouldn't have too long to wait. Her pants hung on the edge of the counter where she'd left them, and she eased herself back into them.

Cutting the vegetables was the boring part but someone had to do it. Her mother was putting the tablecloths on the tables while cleaning and arranging the dining area to her satisfaction. Once that was done Eleanor would start on her pies. Blueberry was the top bestseller but none of her pies were ever left by the end of the day.

Turning the heat on, she placed the pot on the stove and stirred lightly. A pinch of salt and pepper, with a touch of other seasoning changed the flavor just enough. Checking over her shoulder to make sure she was alone; she couldn't resist a little taste. Elena was the only member of her family to partake of the food they prepared. It had remained her secret but had almost been uncovered on a couple occasions. She hadn't always harbored a taste for human flesh and as she cooked her mind began to wander.

* * *

Jameson and Gabe had just returned from their "outing" and had brought in a woman who looked to be in her early thirties. This was their fifth time, and it was becoming easier with practice. They were beginning to perfect a routine. Jameson and Gabe found and brought in the meat. Eleanor and Elena worked on the appetizers and desserts. The preparation of the meat was left to Jameson. He had the stomach for it. Gabe was the one given clean up duty. A messy but necessary part of the process.

Her mother's arms were covered in flour and dough. "Elena, tomorrow's special is the stew. Would you mind getting the base for the soup? I'm behind with these pies."

With a quick nod, Elena grabbed a large pot, and stopped at the knife rack. This was the first time her mother was entrusting this task to her. A surge of pride and confidence swelled within her, and her eyes lit up as she withdrew a slender, five-inch blade.

Her brother and father passed her in the hallway without a word. A look of concentration was displayed on Jameson's face that played in direct contrast to Gabe's look of resignation. A part of him didn't agree with what they did but he was too afraid of their father to ever say or do anything against his will.

Emotions were something that Elena seemed to lack. At least when it concerned her feelings towards the people they murdered. She felt no sadness or remorse over any of it. She was her father's daughter through and through having inherited his gift of lacking a conscience.

The woman's head remained down as Elena crossed the threshold, tools in hand. She couldn't help but pout a little. It wouldn't be fun unless they were awake. Elena was patient to a certain extent and if the woman didn't wake momentarily... there were persuasive ways that came to her mind.

Lifting the woman's head showed a darkening bruise over the left side of her face. Jameson must have done or said something to irritate Gabe. Pressing with her fingers, not so gently, brought a weak groan from the woman and her head moved away.

"There we go," she whispered.

Blond hair obstructed her face as her head went back down.

"Oh no you don't," Elena declared, as she lifted the woman's head.

One slap rocked her head to the side and brought her fully awake. The fierceness in the woman's eyes forced Elena back a step. She was accustomed to fear, desperation, or confusion emanating from their victims but not resilience. Had she not been so taken aback and temporarily shocked, she may have predicted what came next.

A thick wad of spit connected with her face. A look of bewilderment came over her face and she was rooted to the floor for a few seconds. Maybe she was wrong earlier to think that she was devoid of any emotion because her stomach churned like a tea kettle with a burning rage.

Forty-five seconds later, the woman was dead. She didn't even have the chance to release a proper scream, just a series of pained grunts and gurgles before her final breath wheezed out. Blood oozed from eight puncture wounds and six slashes across her stomach, breasts, and neck. With a morbid fascination, she watched the light vacate her eyes and simultaneously felt the anger drain away from her.

The bloody knife fell from numb fingers to clatter noisily on the floor. She'd never lost control before. She cocked her head to the side as a disconnected calm came over her.

Apparently, she was capable of emotions just not sympathy and compassion. Anger came quite readily to her.

Her senses returned and she rushed forward with the pot she had dropped in her explosion of murderous rage. She had multiple options for placement of the pot, but her concern was the blood running out. Content with the blood she'd collected, Elena experienced another first. Worry. Her father was going to be livid. A waste of perfectly good meat.

Maybe not.

If she called for her father maybe he could work fast and get what was needed. She wet her lips and a coppery taste filled her mouth. Some of the woman's blood had sprayed onto her. Lines and dots of red decorated her clothes and body.

To her surprise, she found herself lifting the pot to her mouth. The urge to drink was too powerful to fight and she gave in. She'd always been somewhat curious as to what it would taste like. Not once had a customer complained so it couldn't be bad. Rivulets of red coursed down her chin unnoticed as she drank.

Footsteps coming down the hall interrupted her twisted taste testing and she hastily put the pot down. Wiping her mouth, she worked up fake tears while fabricating a story in her mind portraying her the victim that would help absolve her of any punishment.

* * *

Relishing in the memory, she started cutting the vegetables for the stew. Another scream at a higher octave brought a crooked smile to her face. It wouldn't be long now before her father presented her with the meat.

* * *

CHAPTER 16

"You've given us quite the night and almost made a mess of things. Not to worry though, this isn't the first time someone's tried to escape."

Jameson's gaze fell on the clock on the shelf to his right. Four am. Still seven hours until opening time. His back was to Dylan as he organized his collection of tools. Eagerness and excitement filled him as he heard the young man moving in his restraints. A look over his shoulder showed he was almost fully recovered from the tranquilizers.

"I like to listen to music while I work. I hope you don't mind."

Hold the Line by Toto filled the silence and he hummed along.

"Kidnapping and torturing people is work for you. Damn, I'd hate to see what you fucks do for fun around here." Dylan mumbled with sarcasm, shaking his head.

Jameson chose to ignore the comment and wiped his knives down one final time.

"You do realize people are going to come looking for me. My friends are probably already on their way here."

A coughing fit took hold of Dylan and he tasted blood in his mouth. Not a good sign.

A deep laugh echoed through the room and Jameson's face reddened as he turned around to face Dylan. He slapped his side, took a breath, and continued his charade of laughter. As the last of the tranquilizer left Dylan's system, it was replaced with a white-hot anger that reinvigorated him and he spoke loud enough to break through the mocking gales of laughter.

"Laugh it up while you can asshole. I may be as good as dead, but I swear to God if I get out of these ropes, I will kill every one of you sick fucks!"

The laughter stopped so abruptly Dylan couldn't help but be unnerved. Dylan licked his lips and refused to avert his eyes from Jameson. For a moment nothing happened. No one had ever spoken to him that way and he was a bit stunned.

"One thing that my kids were taught early on was respect. A lesson that you obviously failed to learn," Jameson said softly as he walked over, a large carving knife held in his hand.

He knelt to the side of Dylan and cut thin lines into the skin of his stomach. Rational thought went out the window along with part of Dylan's sanity as he realized this could be the end.

"Normally I use a marker for this part but because you're one mouthy son of a bitch, I figured this method would be more appropriate."

Jameson's attention was solely on outlining the sections of meat he was going to remove. Every few seconds he would use a clean rag to wipe away the blood, so his vision wasn't obscured. Dylan's head collided with Jameson's face in a wet smack. Holding the left side of his face, Jameson staggered away. No broken nose but Dylan was satisfied at what little pain he could dish out.

"Most people beg for their life, cry, or whimper which can make this slightly bothersome," Jameson said in a slightly amused tone. "You continue to resist and fight, which is going to make this next part more fun than usual for me."

The knife plunged into Dylan's side and began to cut downward. The breath expelled from his lungs in a pain-filled scream. With one hand Jameson tugged down on the skin and muscle, as the other continued carving. Dylan's eyes rolled back in his sockets as Jameson stripped a six-inch piece of his stomach away and placed it on a sheet on the metal tray. Jameson measured it at two inches thick.

"Perfect. Two more pieces should just about do it."

* * *

CHAPTER 17

Thirty minutes later

Eleanor strode into the storeroom searching for more dough and flour for her pies. She did her best to ignore the heavy, labored breathing from behind her. The faster she moved, the sooner she could leave the room. There was a reason they each did their own parts. She didn't have the ability to do what her husband did. The screams of pain would stop her. The nosy part of her directed her eyes to the chair in the center of the room.

Sweat dripped from his brow, mixing with blood as it coated his chest. His black jacket was torn, and his leather pants were ruined. Blood leaked from the horrendous wounds and ran down the drains in the floor he was seated above. There were three significant hunks of meat missing from his abdomen that Jameson would use for the special of the day, aptly named "Jameson's Catch". Dark red gauze, previously white, was packed into the three deep wounds: two on his sides, and one in the middle of his stomach. The gauze was to keep him from bleeding out on them and being of no further use. Something they had learned the hard way early on in their endeavors.

It was amazing how much pain and suffering the body could endure and still function. The pain had to be excruciating. Eleanor wasn't sure how aware he was or if he was even awake. If he was still conscious, he probably begged for death with each shaky breath.

Ingredients in hand, she made her way to the door, but a

whisper halted her as she opened it.

"Why... don't... you... just... kill... me?"

"I promise it will be over soon. Just close your eyes and go to a happy place in your mind. Somewhere that you loved as a child," she said in a soothing tone.

His chin dropped to his chest either in defeat or exhaustion. She couldn't be sure which one. Closing the door behind her, Eleanor hustled into the kitchen and bumped Elena with her hip as she passed.

"He's fading fast, but I've got to finish these damn pies. Can you go in there and get enough blood for the Gator Bite sauce please? And do try not to make a mess sweetheart. I need you being the hostess for the morning."

With a bounce in her step, Elena picked up a thin knife along with two medium pots and headed to the back room.

* * *

Wasting no time, she placed one bowl in his lap and tilted his head back gently so that his head rested on the back of the chair. Elena walked behind him and crouched down, resting her chin on his right shoulder. She caressed his head, trying to lure his eyes open. His eyelids fluttered a few times.

"That's it," she urged, kissing his forehead then brushing her lips lightly against his.

Her hand checked for his pulse. Faint, but there. With one hand she lifted the pot up level with his chest. The other rested the blade against his exposed throat. She could feel the bristles of his five o-clock shadow scratch against the back of her hand.

"I'll make it as quick and painless as possible," she lied into his ear.

* * *

CHAPTER 18

8:00 AM

Stale coffee, expired breakfast sandwiches and a cashier with an attitude created one hell of a combination for Warren. Three hours after responding to the call had resulted in nothing but unanswered questions and frustration. The footprints next to the wrecked car were not easy to follow and still didn't explain where the hell the guy had gone. Inquiring to dispatch if any other officers had any glimpse of this Dylan Masterson had only sent his mind into more of a frenzy. People just didn't disappear without a trace. This was real life not some fucked up horror movie.

Something didn't sit right with Warren, and he couldn't quite pinpoint exactly what it was. Mac didn't seem to care and wasn't happy with the idea of digging deeper. As far as he was concerned, it was someone else's problem now. Their shift was over.

"Seven fifty-eight."

Even the cashier's voice caused his neck to spasm in anger.

"Really? That's got to be a mistake," Warren replied, looking at the old sandwich, coffee, and bag of bugles that Mac insisted he get.

"No mistake dude. That's the total. Pay it or leave."

His attention was engrossed in the latest issue of Playboy he had open behind the counter. Warren could have had his service pistol in the kid's face and not gotten a reaction. He hadn't looked up once since the bell over the door announced

Warren's presence.

The impact of his hand on the counter caused the cashier to jump and knock the magazine off the counter. Warren leaned partway over the counter and roughly grabbed him by the front of the shirt.

"Listen closely you stupid, unaware son of a bitch. I've had a long week, been up all night, and I'm not in the mood to deal with your bullshit. I get enough of that from work. Either your register is reading the barcode wrong, or you just don't know what the fuck you're doing."

Warren pulled the punk's face down to look at the items on the counter so he could get a close view before shoving him back against the opposite end of the counter. Racks fell from the display wall, spilling cigarettes, lighters, chewing tobacco and pamphlets for vacationers everywhere.

"There's a police discount. It's on the house. My apologies sir," the kid said, out of breath.

Warren would regret losing his temper later, but currently he felt terrific. It felt amazing to release all his pent-up rage from the past few hours.

"I appreciate it," Warren said, gathering up his items as the bell dinged signaling the arrival of another customer.

Without another word, he walked past the newcomer hardly sparing a glance. Tossing the bugles at Mac, Warren started the car and backed out of the gas station.

"Was he any help?"

"That asshole in there wouldn't have noticed if the building fell down around him."

"So, what's our next move?"

There was only one place to stop to refuel, grab a bite to eat, or rest on the Alley and they were currently at it. Its location was approximately seven miles from the site of the

Mustang.

"This isn't your typical drunk driver scenario. He didn't magically grow wings and fly away. The blood on the ground near the vehicle and the chewed-up tires are bugging the hell out of me."

Warren slowed as an older looking restaurant came into view. A sign near the side of the road dubbed the place 'Hunger Pains'.

"I guarantee you they've got better food than this shit," Warren said, tossing the unappetizing breakfast sandwich out the window as he pulled in. "How do you feel about some good home cooking?"

* * *

THANK YOU TO THE READER

So you've made it to the end...

Hope I didn't gross you out to bad but I wanted to take the time to thank you for coming with me on this journey. This book wrote itself extremely fast. I had the first draft completed in two and a half weeks and then of course the re-writes and editing process began. Originally I finished this novella in early 2016, then took a hiatus from writing until late 2021. Returning to my passion has been so fulfilling and I'm glad that you all were equally as excited about me immersing myself fully back into it. At least those of you who told me you were!

A huge thank you to all of you who have purchased this book and supported me on my journey; you all are amazing! If you all enjoyed this story, be sure to continue on for a sneak peek at the sequel, coming out very soon.

READ ON FOR A SNEAK PEEK AT "FOR HERE OR TO GO"

Prologue

May 17th, 1996

White. It was the color that surrounded and suffocated her for 23 hours each day. The one-hour temporary reprieve which permitted her to walk around a thirty by thirty square, concrete slab did little to ease her anxiety and loneliness. Leg shackles combined with handcuffs through a waist chain severely restricted her movement. There were two phones installed on the wall to the right of the door that opened into the rec yard but wouldn't benefit her due to the limits placed upon her by the judge. The volleyball net that was used by the females in general population was taken down prior to her scheduled rec time, which only fueled her hatred of this place.

Her first week at the prison had been eye-opening, frightening, and painful for the officers who were assigned to her rotation. Deputy Rogers was given a broken nose, two fractured ribs and part of her cheek bitten off from her first encounter with Elena. Severe restrictions had been placed on any and all movement, and interactions concerning her. Even her meals were served to her in confinement, through the metal food flap. The first three days she'd been allowed to eat in the chow hall, at a table by herself and apart from the other inmates but at least she'd been in sight of them.

She hated to think of how long she would be forced to endure it. The silence was deafening and combined with the isolation from the other unfortunate souls that inhabited the prison, she wondered how she had managed to not kill someone during her incarceration.

Not to mention the effect on her already unstable mental state. Did having full length conversations with oneself point the arrows towards the end destination of insanity? Possibly. The concrete cell she now called home was dull, to say the least. A metal toilet, sink, green smock, old ratty blanket and mattress were what occupied her cell. Due to the nature of her crimes and her homicidal, violent tendencies, all other amenities were forfeited. The first few nights had found her curled up on the flat mattress, in the fetal position, as tears rolled down her face. Not remorse for the things she'd done, just a frustration and sadness by how everything had turned out.

How had it gotten so fucked up?

The answer was clear enough but she shied away from it, not giving the mocking voice in her head the satisfaction. The night Gabe had brought in that younger musician, Dylan, was the catalyst that brought about her family's downfall. Tears threatened to come as she thought about the events of that day. Things had turned ugly and bloody.

Footsteps echoed outside her cell brought her mind back to the present, and she knew who was here to see her again. Visitors were a privilege she was not allowed, but the no visitors rule was a joke with her. Friends were a luxury she'd never had anyway. These men approaching weren't just some random people from the street. It was the two detectives from the previous afternoon. The information they'd had at their disposal was sketchy, mostly theoretical, full of holes, and lacked the vital information that only she could give. The statements of the officers on scene were taken at face value due to all of the shock and confusion. The number of victims they'd originally reported was fourteen.

If only that was the case.

It was upwards of thirty five that she could recall. The faces of all of them manifested behind her closed eyes on a regular basis but failed to bring about any feelings of guilt. If anything, reliving those moments helped pass the time and gave her a sense of satisfaction and pleasure.

She hopped to her feet as the lock on the food flap disengaged with a clank. It wouldn't do good to appear weak or beaten down in front of them. She was damned if she was going to let them see that this depressing white hell got under her skin like a festering splinter.

"Let's go Elena. Your friends are here to see you again," the deputy said, holding a pair of handcuffs in her hands.

With a smile she sniffed once, not willing to give Sanchez the satisfaction of the response she so clearly craved. The other officer was a male, T. Roberts according to his vest, and kept both hands placed in front of him, and his eyes were daggers directed in her direction as Sanchez placed the handcuffs on her. A few days prior she'd given him quite the kick to his most sensitive area and he was not going to make the same mistake again. The beating she'd received was worth the look of pain plastered on his face.

"Sanchez to Controls, open cell 6," Sanchez stepped back as the door clicked and opened slowly.

With a wink, she blew Roberts a kiss as she walked past.

It made her happy to see his jaw clench in anger. It wasn't hard to see that he was turned on by her the first time he'd laid eyes on her. He was in his early twenties and she'd seen his eyes rove over her on prior occasions. The things she would do to him if she were given the chance.

"You and I could have some real fun together. A bloody good time."

* * *

CHAPTER 1

The dripping had lessened considerably during the last twenty minutes. Shuffling and voices from the other side of the door could be vaguely heard, but inside the store room only the occasional drop on the floor disturbed the eerie silence. Most of the room was blanketed in darkness. Had there been windows, the sun would have provided some illumination of the carnage. The light seeping in from underneath the door was weak and barely penetrated the dark. It had taken a few minutes for her eyes to adjust to the dark of the room.

Another drop fell on the already slick floor.

Lying on her back, Elena looked upwards at the lifeless eyes that stared back. Lifting her hand, she touched the pale, cold skin of his face and smiled warmly.

"Don't look so down. We had our fun didn't we handsome?"

Shifting slightly on her back produced strange, squelching sounds. The bottom of her cream colored shirt and ripped blue jeans were soaked through. Another drop fell next to her face adding to the steadily growing pool of blood that she was lying in.

The drain underneath the chair did wonders for keeping the floor empty of fluid buildup but not when it was intentionally blocked. A blood stained, black shirt covered it, shoved into the holes to keep the drain from working properly. Elena tilted her head to the side so that she would be able to catch the next fat drop of blood on her tongue. It landed with a plop sending shivers of delight coursing through her body.

* * *

Sitting on the counter in the kitchen, Gabe gnawed lazily at a carrot while occasionally stirring the port that was steaming next to him. The things he did erased any hopes for him to have a taste for meat.

His mother had just finished the last of the pies for the day and was washing her hands. She was an obsessive hand washer. He could recall several times where she'd washed her hands to the point of bleeding raw. Stress tended to do that to a person. A clanking from outside and the sound of the hose meant that Jameson was washing his tools outside. Expecting perfection, he didn't trust anyone else to clean his tools. A firm believer that if one wanted something done right, one must do it themselves. Bleach and other cleaning supplies cluttered one of the shelves behind the work bench. He would take his time as he stripped his tools of all traces of anything human

"Would you mind taking these pies to the fridge to cool down?" Eleanor asked, motioning to the four finished pies next to her. Two pecan, one apple, and one peach cobbler.

Hopping down, Gabe took one in each hand, balanced the other two on each arm, and headed to the store room. They needed a couple of hours to get to the right temperature before being served to the customers. Being careful to not drop the pies, he approached the door rear first, opening the door with his back, and nearly dropped the pies at the disturbing sight in front of him.

Elena was kneeling in a pool of blood, making out with

the dead body. He almost gagged as the kiss continued for longer than necessary. He knew his sister was teetering on the edge of full blown psychotic and trying to deny it wasn't working anymore.

Gabe deposited the pies on the rack next to him and rushed over to his sister. He yanked her to her feet, separating her from the corpse.

"What the fuck are you doing?"

The hose was still running which was a good sign. Gabe was the only one who knew how sick and twisted his sister was. If Jameson knew that Elena harbored certain tendencies and desires... he would blow his top.

"You know what dad would do if he walked in here and saw this? You've got to be more careful sis. What were you thinking?"

She smiled innocently and shrugged her shoulders as blood dripped down from her hair, face, and shirt.

"Go clean yourself up before dad comes in."

Without a word, she hurried out of the room, avoiding the kitchen and her mother, as she crept her way to her room. Picking up the pies, Gabe put them in the fridge like he'd originally intended before intruding on his sister's perverted fantasy. He looked at the clock above the work table. Just under two hours until the first customers started showing up.

With a disgusted grunt, he bent down and yanked the bloodied shirt from the drain, allowing the blood to escape. His sister was seriously fucked up but he considered it his job to protect her, from herself and their father. Gabe couldn't ignore the fact that Elena was getting progressively worse. He tossed the ruined shirt into the corner, leaving it to deal with later.

There was no question that the man in front of him was no longer in the realm of the living. He pushed the man's head back, cold and clammy, as he took out his knife to cut the ropes from his legs and arms. Gabe didn't want the body to fall into him. He would need to work in a timely fashion to get this next part done.

The part of the process that he dreaded most and had never gotten used to.

The hack saw sat in its normal resting place on his father's work table, next to the box of black trash bags. This was the one tool that Jameson allowed Gabe to use in order to perform the task that he had no desire to do himself. So he delegated it to his son. Quick, shallow breaths through his mouth was the key to keeping himself from vomiting as he started cutting above the knee.